All Over Again

All Over Again

Heena Kewalramani

PARTRIDGE

A Penguin Random House Company

To order additional copies of this book, contact
Partridge India
000 800 10062 62
orders.india@partridgepublishing.com

www.partridgepublishing.com/india

About the author

Banker by profession, dancer by passion and writer at heart, that defines Heena Kewalramani.

Great ability to pen down words that create a quick link between the reader and her.

Anything emotion that she quotes will drag into a world where stepping out seems a task.

This is her first book, but we are sure you shall come across some tears with lots of giggles as you read on.

A resident of Pune, alumnus of St. Mira's Girls School And College, she is currently pursuing her Diploma in Taxation Laws with Ness Wadia College of Commerce, Pune.

As I pen down our story; I cry, I smile, I stumble, I rise but with every emotion it's you whom I see.
And that's something that has never changed throughout.

-HEENA

..PROLOGUE

She is a firm & muscular frame of five feet six inches, angular features, long hair, pretty shy girl who thought n' number of times to talk to anyone. Staying alone all the time, or being with books around was something very usual for her. Back then being a best dancer was her only dream. She cooked & her family loved her experiments. She always thought her small dreams, surrounding atmosphere were enough for her.

Then Vihaan, a little less than six feet, a lot more proud of his length, oodles of attitude, sharp featured, fair complexion with black eyes, chubby & loves playing pool & snooker stepped in her life. She felt that he would be like just another person who would stay for some while around and then walk away with time. But he stayed back long and changed her life.. And changed her too…it looked like her life was just waiting for him to step in and change the 'world'. Within no time they became best of friends. She was a reserved girl but with him she shared every bit of her life & could relate with him very easily. He calls her 'FATTU' & she calls him 'TEDDY'.

On the other side he understood her very well. Without telling him much he got to know what she went through, what she wanted.. Just everything. He was always around. Any problem, any matter he was always available for her, come what may.

He helped her relive life again and made her realize what she actually wanted to be but couldn't be. With time his importance changed a lot for her. Their relation also changed. She gave up her one only dream that meant her LIFE to her since childhood.. DANCE… because more than

Vihaan nothing else mattered. Today that she is able to quote poems is just because of him. Due to his love, care, trust, affection she started knitting my feelings into words that spell bounded their relation to another level.

He loved it when she wrote extra senti poems for him. For her the poems were not that great but for him they were very precious. He often told her, "Trisha you know you can be a writer." & she said "I don't want to be a writer for others, it's just my passion of writing these poems just for "you and only you".

When they had tiny fights just like any other relation, she didn't know how to convince him, it was her poems that helped her in resolving the matter. Her poetry started just because of him so she sweared to herself, other than him no one else shall be able to read her poems. Unfortunately, their relation detoriated. He parted ways but love alone played its game. They survived being together after five terrible break ups & two years of separation. Now they are friends again & call themselves "JUST FRIENDS" but both are completely aware that they can never be friends. It's just like saying they are hanging between two relations, neither a couple nor best friends but between the two. She stopped quoting poems after breaking up but then to remember the old times she still writes.

..THIS BOOK WOULD HAVE BEEN IMPOSSIBLE WITHOUT..

A arav, without whom this journey of life wouldn't have started. Janvi who always stood by me without any Conditions apply tag. She is the one with whom I never fought for more than half a minute. Its 5 years now and we are together without cracks in our f'ship.

Kavya who knows me, believes me & my intuitions, my love.

Mit for being Mr Advicer & being a reliable source always.

A heartfelt thanks to authors like Durjoy Datta, Nikita Singh, Ravinder Singh whose books have inspired me to pen down a story and made me beleive that its good to pat the back of budding creativity and let it grow.

Last, but not least my parents who haven't heard great stories from me but believed their daughter's instincts and talent.

...JAB WE MET

I met him in Wadia College when I was there for my F.Y.J.C. admission. I didn't know the procedure for admission conducted there. It was my di who gave me his reference. We knew each other from our childhood days but we were the ones who never spoke to each other because I was a quiet shy little girl and was usually busy studying and he was the completely opposite one; naughty, mischievous and never interested in studies.

We met when he came to my di's place for TUTIIOONNSS' you see (this is because he never studied and just did masti with my cousin and got screwed for the same). The day before we met in the college I ringed him up to know what time should we meet there but sad to say he didn't answer it & due to that I was too angry and felt that this guy had tons of attitude.

Somehow I managed to get the time fixed and then in the college I behaved as if he was a guy too elder to me so used words like 'aap' 'ji' unaware that he is just some months elder to me. That day passed and was just an unfruitful day. Nothing was so special about it to boast about and had no memories to carry forward.

..MUJHSE DOSTI KAROGE

S ome days later when I was relaxing and enjoying the lovely weather outside, rains were pouring heavily, coffee mug in hand on my favorite window in my room, I got an unexpected message on my cell from the same fellow (no special preference as I never liked him because of the attitude and carelessness reflected from his behavior). The message was on friendship day 3rd August asking me to be his friend... and let me not forget that forward with friendship request was just lovely. After thinking for a while I said yes... I thought it would just be a 'hi bye' sort of thing but we really got very well with each other... *ajeeb na.....*

We started chatting with sharing views about each other when we exchanged our looks while passing by in his society...

Me: "When I looked at you I felt that you're arrogant, full of attitude, etc etc...

He said that he too felt that I have attitude. The way I walked in his society was like a QUEEN entering... I was happy to be called like that. But then I assured him that I didn't have attitude, it was just that I was too scared to walk in front of all the society guys so I had to act as I'm really someone from whom all should stay away for safety.

..GETTING CLOSER

T hen everyday was just something that we spent in sending forwards and long chats. We spoke things that no one else in our lives knew about it. Step by step knowingly unknowingly we got too close to each other; we didn't realize that we spent hours of late nights' chatting with each other... We did cross 4am at times...

There was a situation when once I had a terrible fight with Sid (temple friend) and I chose to give Vihaan a call (this was the first time after our friendship we actually spoke to each other on a call) and tell him how badly I was hurt and needed someone to understand what I was going through. After listening to all my talks he said in a typical filmy way *"tere moti jaise aansu bhaut keemti hai uss na samaj bandar ke liye mat gavah.. us ke liye sambhal jo teri kadar kare.. jo tujhe samjhe"*.

That was most amazing line he said. (I know it's often repeated in movies in various styles but the way he said was just mind blowing).

After sharing my feelings with him I felt good not knowing why... I was wondering why did I feel good, just because I shared what was in my heart or something else... later I sent him a thank you message to let him know that I felt good talking with him... but he didn't accept my thanks as he said

"There is no space for sorry... thanks...please...between friends" which in turn again made me smile after shedding a bucketful of tears on that silly fight.

..CONFUSION STARTS

One fine day just while chatting casually he told me that once he had a crush over me and the friendship that started was just due to the same. I forgot this as the chat ended. Then as days passed with it I started getting closer to him not understanding WHY??????

Then next evening I gave him a call as I needed his textbook. He told me he'll come home to give me but as I already had some work at my aunt's place I landed up in his society and that sweet poor little fellow was waiting down in my society premises. Then he too came to aunt's home to make my work simpler.

That day itself in the morning I had dedicated a caller tune to him, I asked him that did he hear it & he replied "NO"

I felt bad at that moment & just said in anger "You know I specially dedicated that caller tune to you." (That caller tune was - bakhuda tumhi ho...from kismat konnection). He didn't react that moment but later when I called him he spoke to me in a different tone & asked "what is wrong with you?"

"What is wrong with me? Matlab?"

"Your uncle was sitting next to you & you were talking to me like this? The way he was staring at me after your sentence. Gosh!! I couldn't even look back at him after that. Why have you dedicated me a caller tune? Why are you getting so impulsive to my presence around you?"

Finally, I told him all the confusion that was there in my mind, what all I was thinking about him, just everything.

I recollected all what I spoke there then I realized what stupid thing I did. I told him sorry and then we decided to chat at night and talk over my 'so confused' situation.

After dinner I texted him what all feelings I had for him, my extra but not so needed concern for him.

I had been listening to songs like "Mera pehla pehla pyar" and "Is this love" and just picturing both of us in the song. And the way still so confused state of my mind is questioning me why I'm I doing this. Then he said

"Dear, can I tell you something?

"Yes"

"You're in love."

"It can't be true."

"Its true, cent percent true."

He gave me a nice big pleasing explanation and then said now we won't chat further as I want you to think over all this. That entire night I couldn't sleep due to two reasons - One do I really love him and second Oh! My God have I really fallen in the most beautiful feeling of love.

Next day in college I approached Kruti.. Tall, sleek, fair, long hair, independent (a good friend) to talk to her everything that happened last evening and night. She too said the same "Baby, you're in love"

I was home after college and thought over all the conversation that started from last evening till date. After exact 24 hours of the first call I called Vihaan again and told him that we need to talk. Then he asked what I wanted to do 'a talk on the phone or meet him personally'

I said we usually talk on phone lets meet tomorrow.

..RIGHTLY SAID A LOT CAN HAPPEN OVER A COFFEE

A fter that my heart started popping with all questions like 'Trishaaa.. ye kya kiya? Milne ke liye bol to diya par kaise milegi, kaha milegi, kya bolegi, kya hoga.....'

New day and a new step in my life. I was meeting a guy whom I knew since childhood, is my friend from last four months, started liking him from last one month *'may be'* but still was shivering like I'm going to watch a horror movie alone.

With all the fear, excitement, happiness ... so many emotions put together I got dressed up in the best possible attire as it was going to be best day of my life as I was to confess my love for someone really close to my heart. We decided the place to meet up. CCD very well known as Café Coffee Day was where I reached with Kruti to meet him (*couldn't go alone.. silly gal*)

..DILLAGI

It was 8th December I reached sometime before he did (*first impression matters na and I was li'l punctual*). Kruti was also going meet one of her friend. I was down waiting for Vihaan. He came after a while wearing my favorite color shirt 'white'. (I was wondering did he wear my favorite color coincidentally or???) We went to the top floor. As I was leading him not understanding what to do I chose a place where we sat opposite to each other. I was still shivering. I started with talks like

"Hi! How are you?"

And he just came to the point (*he understood me very well so knew it that directly starting the topic from my side was impossible*). I told him that before we come to the conclusion I want to know what are you're feelings for me.

While we were talking to each other Kruti's friend commented on me saying

"After going home this girl is going to cry badly"

Even Vihaan felt the same.

Vihaan accepted that he did like to talk to me and the feelings I had for him he too had the same.(*really?? Did I hear it right?? Can someone really pinch me*)

Meanwhile I tore the tissue its due to my consciousness and he made a comment on it.. "Why are you so nervous, I'm not a stranger *I guess,* nor I'm I going to eat you up...Bichara tissue.. Look at it you've hurt him so badly" and after long hours of worry I had a smile on my face so did he. We then started discussing about our past as we wanted each other to know about it as there should be no issues related to them later and more over we believed in transparency. Some tears with some smiles after the past stories ended. It was time for two of us to leave but the conclusion of what is our relation going to be further was still unanswered. *Are we going to be friends or more than that...?*

I told him my state of mind that was conflicting between 80%YES - 20% NO, so I still need to think over it. He too felt the same thing and wanted me to take enough time to think over it as it's a very important decision. We then bid goodbye to each other and left.

On the way back home I noticed the moon(my closest friend with whom I shared things & asked plenty of questions and got answers too with different kind of signs) and sun together in the sky and gave an unnecessary smile to which Kruti said "Trisha why are you smiling so much and what conclusion you two came up to."

I told her what I was feeling.

"I realized that Vihaan is made for me. We two share some very special feelings for each other and it's not just friendship."

That moment it started drizzling and once more I had different kind of smile on my face. (*I thought this too is a sign.. may be what I just said was right. He is the one for me..*)

As I reached home I texted him to inform him that I have reached home safely (that extra care could be noticed that the other person is fine) and I had taken my decision but would disclose it on 31st but he insisted to be disclosed that night itself.

I spent entire evening remembering the moments we spent together and was just waiting for the night to come and then we could again chat and reveal our decisions.

Time passed but it seemed too long (this is obvious to happen when you're in love and can't wait to talk to your loved one). As usual after dinner we started chatting. The first question was same as usual

"Did you have dinner?" and the other replied "Yes, I had and what about you?" then we continued with how was the time we spent together and what was the best and worst moment.

The best moment for both was when we told each other about our not so happening past (it showed that we want to keep the relation true and unhidden) and no moment was bad. Then it was the time to reveal decisions for which we were waiting anxiously.

I texted him

"I feel you're the one made for me and as I have found you I don't want to lose you as you're really precious to me"

He then replied "I want you to give me a call just now and say those three magical words & then you can disconnect the phone and that will make this day complete and perfect for me."

I being so shy girl didn't agree to it. I requested him that I would message him what he wanted to hear but he disagreed. I made excuses; no, my family members would hear my voice and come in my room and scold me. The next one was my grandma is sleeping in my room I can't do this. With the excuses I messaged him those three magical words every time.

But nothing worked and he was upset with me & I didn't like it (*this was to happen as the relation didn't even start and this was happening but ruthna manana are a part of love relations na*) he knew all excuses that I made were fake just to avoid saying the three words. (*he knew everything that went on in my mind well, could understand me like no one else*)

But finally he said it's ok I'll manage with the message this time but next time no excuses. It was just a wonderful day for both and the night had to be over the blues. It was 9th December (*the confession was after 12 am that's why date changed*) when we actually confessed that we were truly in love each other. (*Amazing na. WOW!!! I'm so happy... he also must be happy na*)

As I see it

I can see lot of life in you.
I can see what I want to.
I can see what you can't.
To be with you, is all I want..

Winter, monsoon, summer.
We'll wither every weather.
Come here, sit with me,
You make everything look better.

When the water pours.
Let's then get wet.
Let's get old together.
Let the sun set.
Let life be simple.
Let me love you.

The next morning I woke up with a smile, remembering yesterdays' every moment and how special it was in all ways. Yeah, I did expect him proposing in the most unique way he could as I was a bad filmy girl. But that wasn't above the best time we had together. It was unique in its own special way. Perhaps, we didn't meet that day being a special one but being in love is like the person is just around you always, every moment. We were in constant touch. Thanks to the one who invented a cell phone that kept us together with every passing second of the day.

The next day I was still a bit unsure about our relation so spoke to Kanika, his's closest friend. I thought I would just get to know him better and clear some silly doubts like

'I'm I being extra conscious or is it just normal'

'I'm I over reacting and stuff'

We had a good friendly chat though we spoke to each other for the first time. She told me about his anger more briefly, certain likes and dislikes. It clearly reflected how close they were that made me jealous. How can I not go through this, he was just mine and how can some other girl talk about him so much???

Apart from that during our conversation I got to know that he had a terrible bad habit of smoking. *"Smoking you know!" Does he even have any idea how I hate every person on this earth who touches a cigarette. I never even spoke to my jiju who had it almost every day.* Kanika often scolded him not to do so but he often flipped of the topic. Me, being his girlfriend got this responsibility to get him out of this. I did promise and then we didn't talk much as my mood completely changed from good to a worse one listening to that crap. I had to hang up as soon as possible to give a call to him and talk.

Called up Vihaan. I loved him so couldn't afford being harsh at first instance. It started as usual 'Hi, how are you' I told him that I spoke to Kanika sometime back. In quick recession he added

"You girls spoke? It means the topic has to be me, my complaints etc..."

I retarded "Yeah, it had to be you. But being true I called her as I was still a bit conscious about our relation but got to know lottss.. about you"

"Like whatttt?" (*voice little shocked*)

"Your likes, dislikes, good as well as BAD part of you." *Yes I did stress on the word BAD.*

"All fine? Tell me too what you two spoke"

"I'm not telling you everything as it's not too important for you to know girl talks. But there is one thing that has hurt me a lot." I said.

His voice suddenly rose as he questioned "What?"

Trying to calm down myself I asked

"You smoke?"

His voice lowered now. "Yes, I do." Trying to interrupt me before I said something. "But, it's very rare. Dear"

"But then why didn't you ever tell me before. The day we first met you told me everything, then why not this." My voice sounded a bit heavy and a bit choked.

"Dear I didn't even touch it since long time"

"Do you know how badly I'm hurt. Sorry to say this but If I would know about this before I wouldn't have ever spoken to you" I sounded too harsh but I was deeply hurt by the one I trusted a lot, above everything.

He too was hurt by the way I spoke, kept quiet for a while but understood what I felt. Then he spoke

"Trisha, I never wanted to hurt you but because I stopped it long back I thought it had no importance left in telling you. And I really don't want to lose you."

His words melted my anger but not my questions. "But what was the need to have them? What tension you have? I think people with tension burdened head prefer having cigarettes' to reduce the pressure. Your parents know about it? What would they feel when they get to know about it? You must have started this silly habit under someone's influence. Some friend of yours. Who is it?"

"Dear please relax… calm down…I just had it due to switching of moods. Rohit used to go so I accompanied him." "Once you know some society uncle saw me puffing. I was so embarrassed you know."

"Now you realize it's so bad." I was normal now. I couldn't be rude to him don't know why. Even after he did a mistake I couldn't be upset for long. I made him swear on me that he would never do it again. Talks changed.

Love is so crazy na you're upset with someone, You don't want to talk to him. You tell him that. And still you wait for the same person to call you or text you so you keep checking your phone repeatedly.

No one was at home so we had long talks. Plans for next meet and what either of us was feeling about the new relation and how badly we missed being together. We spent hours in CCD on our favorite corner seat. I used to go there with my friends before I met Vihaan, where we all friends shared some fun filled moments. I bunked hours of my college lectures and he missed his favorite pool games to be with me.

..RAB NE BANA DI JODI

It was the fourth day of our relation. He asked me out for a movie "Rab ne bana di Jodi" starrer being The Great SRK 'Sharukh Khan.' Vihaan knew it very well that he was my favorite actor so he planned accordingly (from just the beginning of the relation he was taking care of my likes and dislikes so well sweet na). The plans started long back. Kanika knew about it and she started teasing us *'perfect movie for the perfect couple at a perfect beginning.'*

Day, timing all fixed. I informed at home I was going college. His call came. One...two...three...times continuously. I couldn't answer as parents were around.

"I'm just leaving" I dropped a message for him. He didn't want to miss the start. Kruti came to pick me and zooommm... we left. He was waiting for me. (I still remember the way he was leaning on the wall, nice pose, eyes on the entrance) I got off the bike and got some do's and don'ts from my friend as she left. We were in then. We sat in the middle row. The movie started. I was with the guy whom I cried, laughed, loved all these days but we didn't speak a word waiting for the other to start. I was sorry for being late he said "It's ok."

"What you told at home?"

"I'm going college"

"Ok..."

He wanted to say something but didn't.

Then there was a scene where the actor learnt dance for his wife.

"Vihaan… can I ask a question?"

"Yes"

(just sitting next to him I didn't have the guts to ask him directly so I messaged him…. ahhhhh such a silly moment)

"You know very well like this actress I'm also crazy about dance, sooooo would you too learn dance for me?"

I thought I was being demanding but then I felt I can ask for it. He's no more a stranger.

He sweetly replied "Why not? Anything for you sweetheart."

I smiled and made myself more comfortable but then as he was trying to come closer my certain move made me him feel that I was still scared of him and getting close was not meant to be. But that wasn't true.

A lovely romantic song started.*(tu hi toh jannat meri, tu hi mera junoon, tu hi toh mannat meri, tu hi ruh ka sukoon, tu hi ankhi yon ki thandak, tu hi dil ki hai dastak aur kuch na janu bas itna hi janu tuj me rab dikhta hai yaara main kya karu.. sajde sar jhukta hai yaara main kya karu.. tujh me rab dikhta hai yaara main kya karu)* Or I would say my kind of song as my friends say it. As per them all senti songs and love songs were *'my kind'* of songs They always called me Ms. Senti. My eyes got a bit wet due to the song.(I was just thinking to what extent Srk went to please Anushka) He understood it well. Later when I couldn't control myself he asked "Your fine?"

"Yes"

"Sure?"

"Yes"

Two minutes passed but I was still the same. He got tensed. He started with same questions and got same replies. Then suddenly he said "Let's go"

I didn't utter a word.

"Kruti said leave a bit early before the movie ends so chalo."

I kind of knew I have spoilt his mood. But had to do what he asked me to. I got up. We left. Suddenly he stopped at the exit. Luckily no one was there. He wanted to hold me, shake me and ask "Kya hua Trisha anything wrong. Have I hurt you or what is it, speak up" but he didn't do anything of that sort... He was too concerned about my tears.

"You're still not fine what happen? The crying scene is over why are your eyes are still wet"

"I'm not crying anymore I'm fine"

There was complete silence for next one minute. He wasn't satisfied with my answer. Then he indicated me to leave.

I was just tying my scarf and he asked "How are you going to college? Kruti is coming or ....?"

"I'll manage. She would be in some lecture."

"I'll drop you"

"No, it's ok"

"Wait here I'll just get my bike" (first order from him)

His order couldn't refuse. That was the first time I was on his bike (*Blue Pulsar; it's still my favorite*). I was sitting behind him with caution and space between us. I wanted to keep my hand over his shoulder to let him know I'm fine but wasn't that bold enough. He then confirmed "You're sure your fine?"

"Chill dear I'm fine. Once I start crying, it's for sure for next sometime I'm still in the same state"

He dropped me a bit away from my college gate. He held my hands. I was shivering. (Everything for the very first time) He was still not convinced and couldn't leave me in such a state.

Are you sure you want to go college like this?

Yes dear, I'm fine. Don't worry. If I need you I'll give you a call.

Ok. Bye take care love you

Love you too.

I went in the college, called up Kruti and told her to come in the parking. I told her everything that happened and how I spoilt his mood. While she was just telling that it's ok it happens when your too sacred or something you tend to make mistakes and don't worry he will understand. This was just the first time you two were alone together so its obvious for you to be a bit scared. Vihaan calling, my phone screen flashed & I took Kruti away from all other girls around. Then I spoke to him.

"I want to meet you now."

"Why? What happened?"

"I just want to meet you now. Tell me where you're coming?"

"Buttttttt whatttttttt's thhheee matteeeerrr"

"I left you in college in that state of yours, I shouldn't have done that. And now I want to see you, change your mood, make you feel better. Soooooo I want to meet you. Any more questions????"

"Naaaa…. Come to CCD I'll see you there in 10 mins. But Kruti too would be there, will that be ok?"

"Sure. No problem"

I told her that we had to go to CCD to meet Vihaan now.

"But why?"

"He said that's why"

"Ok fine let's go"

There we reached. Looking at me he gave a smile.

"What happened to you? All fine Vihaan" Kruti asked.

"I'm fine just got too worried after leaving Trisha with that sad face. I couldn't concentrate on playing pool also. So I thought its better I would meet her again for a while to change her mood to a better one."

"Ok.. You're sure you want to change her mood? Or you want to change your mood by seeing her smile.. ha?"

There comes a shy smile

We all then sat on our favorite place upstairs.

Both Kruti and Vihaan were making fun of me and were talking about the way I behaved during the movie and that made be bit upset and I was also trying to reply back in the same tone.

Somehow my mood changed. It was most of the time that he and Kruti were talking but still I was having my conversation with him at the same time.

You must be wondering 'HOW?'

Aankhon hi aankhon me hmmmm…

Then it was time to leave as I was getting late for home.

I went downstairs before Kruti and Vihaan and paid the bill. I did so because I felt in a relation there is nothing called as you or me it's us.. But unfortunately when Vihaan went to the bill counter and got to know that I have already paid the bill he got VERY upset with it.

That moment he just gave me a frown look but didn't say anything. Evening when were talking to each other he scolded me for the bill issue.

"What's the big deal? It's ok"

"It's not."

"You pay, I pay same thing na"

"Not this. I don't like when the girl pays when the guy is with her"

"Ok teddy (I loved calling him this because of two reasons- one I loved soft toys and second he was actually like a teddy; sweet chubby-chubby")

Everything just worked after that Teddy word. All his frustration over me was drowned.

"Your very smart…when you tell me Teddy and talk like a kid I just forget all my anger over you. And due to your sweetness I can't stay angry with you for a long while"

"Thank you thank you….i know I know how sweet I am"

"Really?"

"Yeah, that's why toh you love me so much na"

After some sweet chats he told me something that I didn't know.

"Trisha you know something?"

"What?"

"We actually got a corner seat for the movie but I thought you wouldn't be comfortable so then I took you to the middle row seat as it was vacant"

Meanwhile I was having thoughts in mind like I wouldn't have any issue if you would take the corner seat and all.

I just said "okkkkkiieess......"

Altogether we two found a different set of happiness. Something we never got before. Just at the beginning we got so much from it unexpectedly.

Kanika and Vihaan often questioned me one thing

"You don't mind na we two talking to each other and stuff"

I always told them "No I don't. You two are just good friends and why would I mind it. I really have no issues."

I too never wanted two good friends to get separated just because of me.

It was 22nd December Kanika's birthday. I was meeting Vihaan as usual after my college. Vihaan and Kanika couldn't talk directly to each other as her boyfriend had certain issues with Vihaan earlier so she was restricted to talk to him. So I called to wish her. I told her that Vihaan too wants to talk but then she was with her boyfriend so they couldn't talk and I wished her on his behalf too.

Vihaan and I were still together. After some while a group of boys and girls came there. Just to tease Vihaan I behaved as though I liked a guy in that group and I told "Vihaan that guy is looking smart na"

"Yeah, really. You want me to go and talk to him for you"

Look at this your own boyfriend is ready to get some other guy for you just if you say 'He's handsome' *Weirdo.*

"Do you have any idea what you just said? I just hope you remember that we are in a relation and how can you talk to me about getting some other guy for me when you're just sitting besides me?"

"Chill… for your happiness I can do this too"

"You know it well where my happiness lies, don't you?'

"You said he's good, smart, nice personality and all so I said that"

"You know it well I was just trying to tease you."

"But I was serious. I can move out of your way if you like some else other than me"

"Stop it Vihaan. I just like you and there is no space for anyone else. I'm saying this now and will repeat when needed"

May be he still felt we were not the ones to be together. My silly joke turned to be a serious talk.

That evening when we were on call in the evening, and again Vihaan asked "You don't mind na, Kanika and me staying in touch, sharing talks and all?"

"No dear. I really don't mind"

But still the questions didn't end and finally I said things that no ever thought I would say nor did I know I would be so harsh.

"I do mind you too talking to each other. I'm jealous etc etc…"

We didn't chat that night..

..FIRST HUG

Next day I was sorry for the last night issue.. That moment I said all in anger but later the way I was weeping was horrible. I met him and apologized.

"Dear, it's ok stop crying. Nothing was intentional, it was just intension. You've cried all night now stop it."

"I'm really sorry"

"You need a hug?"

I nodded

And he hugged...I buried myself in his chest..

"You know you look like a kid when you cry.. cute"

I was just replaying everything that happened past all these days and was feeling like me being a fool. First there was a scene due to the movie and now this thing which would have created differences between two friends. I was feeling sorry for such silly behavior of mine. I met him next day to explain everything. I said sorry to him and komal too.

It's said na 'When the end is well, all is well'

That thought was there in my mind. But I was still upset with myself.

A thought by Vihaan for me

"I HATE TEARS AS THEY MAKE
YOU SAD,

I LOVE TEARS CAUSE THEN YOU
SNUGGLE UP IN MY CHEST &
COME MORE CLOSER TO ME."

...YEAR ENDING

3 1st night was coming. A new year was waiting ahead to start. Vihaan decided that we would be together on this day. I was eagerly waiting for the eve.. finally he gave a call and it was decided to meet, no where else but are common favorite place CCD. I wanted to look my best for my sweetheart so I delayed time in getting ready and in hurry I forgot to text him that I'm leaving. Gave him a call when I was just about to reach and….

Hey dear I'm so sorry dad isn't allowing me to go out.

Why?

It's 31st so checking is going on everywhere and I don't have gear bike license so might fall into trouble as per dad.

OKK. Actually I'm about to reach.

Where are you right now?

KP dear.. It's ok… We'll meet tomorrow morning.

No you're not going back I'm coming just give me some time I'll do something

But dear dad is right I don't want to see you in trouble cause of me.

Nothing will happen I'm coming. Just sometime and I'll be there.

I reached CCD. I was entering alone for the first time.☹ but I knew in some while he'll be with me.

The waiter recognized me well till now as Vihaan and I often went there together. Not as usual but our favorite place was reserved by some other group. Time was passing slow and I wasn't feeling good. There was

34

a group next to me. Amongst them a guy was staring at me continuously and it made me feel me more uncomfortable.

Finally Vihaan was there. I scolded him for making me wait for so long. Then he said I'm sorry & now tell what's the actual problem?

I was stunned. How could he understand that I'm not angry coz he came late.. it was because of the other guy I was feeling restless. I told him the problem, he got very angry & was just about to react but luckily the group left within another fraction of seconds.

Then it was my turn to get scolding's.

"Who told you to wear such an outfit?(I was wearing a sexy top with a stole and my favorite pair of jeans)"

"Possessive ha..(I was enjoying it)"

"Look at you, you are smiling."

"I was so worried whether I would be able to meet you or no and you.."

"Ummmhmmm"

"You shouldn't wear something like this when you're alone.."

"Ummmm..."

"What hmmm??? I'm a fool saying rubbish things"

"Chill sweetheart I'm just admiring how much you care for me.."

"You know it well when you smile like this I can't hold on my anger."

☺ I know it that's why I keep smiling

Then we shifted to our favorite place that was vacant by now.. and there comes a hug but before we could get more close my phone rang *(this phone has to ring always on the wrong time)*

Mum calling.

I answered and…same old questions when you will come home and all.. she told me to wish my friends happy new year…

After the disconnecting the phone..

Happy new year in advance…

Itna jaldi?

Mom ne bola apne friends ko wish kar meri taraf se.

Ohh!! I see.. meri saas ne wish kiya…thank u thank u.. :p

He came close to me. I had so many to things to talk to him but I felt numb. I could speak nothing. The very moment I saw I him I was lost in his eyes. Usually a guy is lost in the girl's eyes and just keeps adoring her but here I was admiring him. I was happy by the end of the year I have someone who loves me so much, can take any risk to be with me, can do anything to make me smile, understand my silence, read through my eyes….. only he was doing the talking & as usual I was just listening.

Finally time arrived when we had to leave. The extended time limit mum gave was also insufficient for two of us. Before we left there was a tight hug and he made sure I tied my scarf and would take care of myself and text him as I reach.

We two were searching for a rick for me but didn't get any. After a long wait he decided he would drop me. We both were not sure about it.. 1st he had no gear license and 2nd what if someone on the way saw both of us. With no option left he said just to assure me that we will take a safer route so nothing will happen, no cops & no other probs.. I knew he was still a little scared but to keep me away from panicking he kept assuring me.

And to keep him distracted I started talking endlessly. The cold was increasing & so was the distance reducing between us. I hugged him tight.

"Trisha, my dad".

"What???? Where??"

"There".

"Where? How will I recognize him? I have never seen him before. How can you be so composed when your dad is here?"

"Aree.. *chari maai* I mean cops not my dad.."

"Silly u scared me."

"Ha.. aur itni der se what are you upto? CCD me aawaz nahi nikli aur ab yaha main tension me hu & you're trying to get close and romantic."

"Arre meri jaan I was trying to make you feel good."

"Really?"

"Ha baba.. & you know it when you keep looking at me I can't speak anything. Now you're not looking at me so advantage for me na...I can go on.."

"Yaha main soch raha where I should drop you and you are talking about advantage."

"Ok I'm disturbing, right? So I better stay quiet."

"Gussa aaya"

"Nahi baba"

"I was pulling your leg.. Shame on you.. Mazak bhi nahi samjta."

"Oye hello.."

"Bolo"

"Nothing"

Between our conversations he was checking out for ricks that would drop me home but no avail.

Almost 5 min away from my home near 11' east street café we found a rick for me. A loose hug and I left. I texted him as I reached home.

The best 31st I ever had. As I entered home I realized mum wasn't well. I texted him and told him that I would chat later as I had to cook, till then he could spend time with his friends.

Due to Mum's health I didn't wanted to go out. But after dinner she insisted I should go for a ride with dad and bro so I left with them. I picked my favorite heart shaped red balloons and choco-choco dip ice cream on the way. While dad was still riding, it was a min left for 12 am. I wanted to talk to Vihaan but couldn't so dropped a voice message for him and it went as.. 'Many many happy returns (*oops I was wishing him for the new year not his birthday*) for the new year.. jaan(I said in my mind)

He immediately replied back.. Same to you sweetheart & don't bite your nails & keep thinking of the tiny mistake you did. It's ok.. something new for me as a new year wish…now smile..

"Love you jaan."

"Love you too sweetheart."

I was home. after that we didn't chat much as I was super tired and needed rest.. so I hugged the balloon thinking that its Vihaan and dozed off to sleep.

1 MONTH ANNIVERSARY

My first relation had completed a month.. Wow what a feeling.. I wished him at 12. I was sure he was planning something special for the next morning. Without delay & full of excitement I winded up all work & got ready on time while humming *(tuj me rab dikhta hai yaara...)* & reached college.

I attended assembly & by that time Vihaan had called me 15-20 times. But due to no network coverage he couldn't catch up with me. After the assembly I got missed call alerts. The last call was from Kanika..

I was completely unaware of what had happened during my assembly & there he was panicking thinking that something had gone wrong with me.

I gave him call & explained that I was perfect & was stuck in the assembly. He told me to join him for lunch but without much thought words spilled out from my mouth saying "NO"

Crashh!! I broke his heart.

I was shocked why I just did that.

later li'l composed I told him I'm not keeping well so can't have outside food.

But the fact was that I was superrr nervous & that meant my sweaty hands, shivering feet.

Even if I wasn't well for him I could have done anything to see his glowing smile but nahh.. I had turned the curve upSide down.

Here I couldn't handle him & there were random calls from Kanika for screwing all his plans.

"Trisha do you have any idea how he had planned the entire day for you today, but bang on what you did huh.. You have hurt him so much. He was going propose you today. Do you even realise that"

Crashh two.. What the hell. What I'm I supposed to do now.

Call Vihaan.

"Hey sweetheart kaha ho?"

"Playing pool"

So when are we meeting?"

"We aren't meeting."

"Hey sweetheart I'm really sorry, darr gayi thi, nervous hogayi thi. I'm sorry"

"It's ok."

"So please now meet me"

"Not now. I'm not in a good mood bye."

"Please na"

"Nope"

"Fine. I'm going CCD. Will wait till you don't come."

"I'm not coming"

"Your wish. But I'm going wait till I don't see you"

Call disconnected.

So sms starts.

"I know I have hurt you once again, but today till I don't see you I'm not going to eat anything nor drink water & will wait till you come.. That's going be my punishment."

I took two flowers for him, yellow & red. Couldn't find white (symbolizes peace)

An hour passed. He still didn't come but I didn't lose hope.

Kruti tried convincing me to eat or go home but I disagreed & asked her to leave me alone.

There he entered after 20- 30 calls.

"You know it well I can't see you crying but still you love to do that. Right?"

"I wasn't crying."

"Look at your eyes they have gone red, your face pale white."

"Good for me. Nice punishment."

"Shut up dumbo"

Waiter interrupted.

"Sir your order?"

"A bottle of water, coffee & pizza."

Waiter: "ok"

Other than sharing the pizza bite by bite, I got a hug and a kiss on my forehead☺

"I'm sorry for hurting you"

"It's ok. By the way muje yaad karte karte rose ke petals tod diye?"

"Na maine nahi kiya. Kruti's friend was fidgeting with it. But fortunately he didn't do anything to the red one"

"Okkkk.. but I'm not taking it with me."

"Why"

"You keep it with yourself as my memory"

(I still have them I in my diary)

We spent next part of the day together.

Seriously this guy was mad. I troubled him so much, hurted him so much but still what all matters to him is my smile.

..PRELIMS

"Environmental exam hai kal."

"Your prepared?"

"Nah. Aage wali ya peche wali dikha degi."

"You're so smart. Can't you study for yourself instead of copying."

"It's a boring subject bacha."

"You're talking as if you study for other subjects."

"See your so smart jaan, you know everything so well. That is the reason I love you so much."

"Ha ha shuru butter lagana. Whenever I talk about studying all you can think is romance that's called smartness."

"Wow. Here your guy is being romantic & you want to talk about books.. shame on you."

"Emotional blackmail ha."

"So what?? Ok tell me when are we meeting tomorrow?"

"After your exam."

"Cool we are meeting at 11am CCD."

"What??? Are you kidding? Your exam starts at 10 & you want to meet at 11?"

"Ha so what. I'm not going to write the entire EVS book in the exam."

"But still."

"No still will. We are meeting at 11."

"Teri baat na manu.. pitna hai kya muje. Fine 11 done."

As I was about to reach CCD I saw him from a distance standing near the parking, leaning over a car bonnet, with a drooping face.

As I went closer to him he gave me a tight hug, we walked in after that without uttering a word.

"Hey sweetheart kya hua? All fine? Exam was bad kya?"

"Nah it was good."

"Then all of a sudden you came & hugged me that too in the parking. Something is fishy. Speak up."

"Nah sweetheart all is fine."

"Enough of your lying (I took his hands in my hands, holding them tight)"

"I can clearly make out your hiding something. When I'm with you, you never do tp with other stuff nor do you look away from me. You're fidgeting with your id, looking down. Bolo na kya hua."

"Exam was good dear but there is some other problem but you don't worry about that. All will be fine soon. You tell me what's with you?"

"Shut up. Don't try to cut off the topic. Tell me the problem."

"Nope I'm not going to tell you."

"But why do you always do this? I always share everything with you. But you never do."

"See dear chill. It's just that I don't want you to take tension."

"Wow your tension can't be my tension but my tension has to be to yours. Sweetheart I hope you remember we are in a relation where all should be transparent. If we can share our happiness then why not our sorrows."

"See dear you know me I don't open up so well. I like to keep my things to myself."

"Fine do as you wish."

"Ok that's enough now I don't want to argue. And don't you dare repeat that line. I hate it & you know it. If the problem is solved I will tell you about it or else I won't."

"As if I want to argue & yeah I won't repeat it. It hurts Vihaan when you don't open up with me. It makes me feel our relation is incomplete & I'm lacking something.

"Jaan it's nothing like that. You are the perfect one for me but please give me some time. I'll try opening up."

"Take your time but don't stretch it too long as you know it will affect our relation adversely. By the way I'm very sorry I fought with you when you're already trying to clear some mess."

"Enough now. No more sorry & all. Give me a big smile so that I can smile too."

"A hug & kiss waves of the tension."

"Trisha can I ask for something?"

"From when did you start taking permission?"

"I want a kiss on my lips."

"NOOOO"

"Why not?"

"After your exams."

"No excuses. I want it now. C'mon it's the first time I'm asking you for some things. Don't you want it too? Don't you want to make my mood?"

"Jaan samja karo. This isn't the place &.."

"And what? I know you're shy but it's ok.. it's me so relax."

"See, you need to go home. Even I'm getting late for dance class. Sir will screw me if I'm not on time for practice."

"Forget sir. And we aren't leaving until I don't get a kiss."

"Muaah"

"Not cheeks. Lips."

After too much argument I had no option.

"But what if someone comes up? It will be embarrassing."

"No one will come. Stop wasting time. Hurry up."

"Muwwaahh" And I hugged him tight. "that's it"

"Trisha, not fair."

"Teeeedddyyy ...Chalo na"

"Fine. ☹ but atleast look at me. Stop hiding your face behind my back. Baap re kitna sharmaegi."

"Love you. Now lets leave?"

"Love you too.. Muwaah (lips)"

That opened my eyes wide enough and a blushing face that he couldn't avoid looking at.

"Now aren't you getting late?"

"ha ha chalo"

The first kiss always remains the best one. All day I could just blush & he would just smile.

..Boards

V ihaan's exams were coming up
     "Jaan we need to stop meeting now"

"Why bacha?

"Your exams are coming, you better start preParing, I don't want you to divert your attention elsewhere."

"Dear that won't happen, I promise."

"No excuses. I'm not listening to you. We can spend maximum time together in vacations."

"But that's not fair. You know it I won't be able to study, will be thinking about you only."

"You haven't even started studying & now only you're saying this. See sweetheart I'll plan your schedule, all will go well. And I have really high expectations from you."

"☹This isn't done"

"All is fair in love & war... so baby this is love.. All will go as I say. Got that?

"Order ha?"

"Yup. Any prob?"

"Do I have a choice?"

"Nope, you don't."

"As you say madam"

"That's better."

"You prepare the schedule later but now can we talk something else?"

"Umm umm.. your birthday is coming."

"I didn't know only."

"Hahaha joke. But.."

"But what Trisha?"

"Nothing. I'll plan that too. It's your first birthday we'll be celebrating together. Wow. Thank God that's after your exams get over."

"Trisha I'm missing you, want to see you right now. come on your window I'm coming."

"Okkk.."

That was the last talk we had. I started planning his study schedule without knowing what was happening at his place.

I called him next eve after receiving no calls or messages all day.

..TROUBLE WAS ROUND THE CORNER

1st call, 2nd call…. 5 calls. But no response. The number your calling is switched off.

I was too worried. What went wrong why is his phone switched off. Any problem?

After an hour I got a call from his landline. But couldn't answer mom was right in front of me.

As mum disappeared from my room I called back on the landline.

With every ring I was just hoping he should pick up the phone & all should be fine.

Hello.

Hi dear. What's wrong? Where is your phone since morning, no calls or messages?

Calm down sweetheart. I'm fine. You remember I had told you that I'm in a trouble if it gets solved I will tell you or else I won't & we had an argument too.

Yeah jaan. But hua kya? Now please tell me what was wrong? And why is your phone off?

V: see first thing don't call back on landline. I will call you whenever possible. I have a caller id on the landline phone so if my parents see that then you will land up in a big time trouble. And I don't want that.

See the scene is like I lended my friend some cash for some reason but he wasn't able to pay back on time so I was very worried all these

48

days as you noticed. I told bro about all this so at least some one in the house would know but he went & told dad & mum everything.. So mum dad are very angry & mum threw away my phone in anger and it broke. I'm not allowed to talk to anyone nor can go out.

Gosh!!! I'm feeling so bad for you sweetheart. I can understand what you're going through. Anyways you better take care of yourself and be calm don't react to anything they say. Just listen to them & concentrate on your studies, if you study they will feel good. And I'm always there for you. Just a call away. Will miss seeing you, but when it's something good for you I'm fine with it.

I'm feeling bad too. I too want to meet you. I hope things get settled soon. Chal I'll hang up before anyone comes.

Bye jaan take care miss you, love you. All the best.

Miss u too sweetheart take care. Thank you.

After that phone call things changed on my Side. I coudn't think of anything else other than him. What he might be feeling, how would things be at his place?

When will I get to see him next?

When parents would go out for some work he would see to it that he could share a word or two to me.

I would also make excuses at home and go to his society to get a glimpse of his bike & he could see from his balcony (he wasn't allowed to step down till exams) one such evening was when I was supposed to attend a party at class I went to his society. There was no current but still he stood on his window to see me.

"You're looking so cute today"

"Thank you but its so dark how you noticed?"

"Pagli, do I need lights around to see you?"

"Point hai."

Normal discussions about his exams & how life without each other was so different.

..BREAK UP??????

H is exams had ended with that many things changed at his place but I was completely unaware of what is coming up.

He was down in society campus when we came across each other.

"Hey jaan"

"Hi dear"

"How are you?"

"I'm good & you?"

"I'm good. Dear we need to give a break to our relation. I'm sorry I'm telling you everything like this but I can't afford hurting you anymore."

"What? Are you serious? Did I hurt you again, what's the reason behind all this?"

"Dear you didn't hurt me. Things have been changing a lot at home after the last issue. Too many restrictions have been coming up so at will be difficult for me to give you time."

"That's ok dear we'll figure out some way but why break?"

"It's just a break not end. Lets' just give sometime to it."

"This is so not happening."

"And one more thing I'm going Bombay after finals so won't be here on my birthday too."

"Vihaan don't do this"

"Please understand me dear. It's equally difficult for me."

"I need some time."

"I understand."

After that call I didn't know what to do. I had no option other than accepting his decision. But it was hurting a lot.

Time was as slow as turtle.. We spoke once a while but it didn't last for hours. I couldn't lose hope so just kept fingers crossed. Finally he said we could meet. I had missed his birthday so thought to celebrate it that day itself. With li'l less time in hand I picked a Belated happy birthday card, some chocolates & cake.

The date I met was him July 27, exactly five months from his actual birth date.

He was quite surprised & I liked that.

..PARTY TIME

August was here, had to plan bro's birthday. I couldn't manage diverting my mind but tried my best. All was set for the next eve party. I was chatting with Vihaan at night & just after normal greetings he said something that made me jump out of the bed.

"Hey dear it's getting really difficult."

"I'm not getting you Vihaan. What are you saying?"

"I think we should get back together."

"Really? Are you serious? I mean I just can't believe my eyes. Did I exactly read it right?"

Once again so many emotions were flowing out together.

We again got together. We were very happy & so was my best friend Jia.

It was just few months we actually started interacting but we shared many common interests & gelled up well.

Vihaan & I were back on track.

Celebrated bro's birthday with double excitement.

.. I GROW LI'L OLDER

B irthday night started with the most precious persons' wish. Vihaan gave a call. Diwali was round the corner. So for a new beginning I started with burning crackers *(burning old memories & seeing the bright sparks of a new life)*. Ma sang happy birthday song in every way possible.

Next morning I got off from all work. All day I was answering calls and his calls were maximum. I took an off from dance class too to meet him. Got an awesome gift. It was difficult to express anything by words, Just needed the right feelings to understand.

Next day ma arranged satsang at home for me so that I could get everyone's blessings.

Learnt some lessons of life *'blood relations can fall weak at times but the relations you make with heart can't back off come what may'*

..WHY FUN TIME & EXAMS CLASH??

It was Gurunanak jayanti. So spent half of the day in temple. While lightning candles in the temple I could have burnt myself to ashes but was always saved & every moment I felt that there is someone on this earth praying for my life & health.

And then it was time I had to study and get back all lectures I gave Vihaan during his exams.

He was more strict than me & I could never argue with him so I always gave up & did what I was told.

..SMILE SMILE ALL THE WHILE

Happy day. Happy moments. Sweet memories arise. Something unexpected. I felt him, he felt me. We felt love, we felt life. We both had smiles but no words to exchange.

Something's' never told but understood is love.

Expressing the glitter is needed at times but then there are times when just a glance says it all.

Vihaan meant a lot to me. I believed a lot in God so to thank him for Vihaan's presence in my life I started fasting on every Chaturti for him. He didn't like when I stayed hungry all day for him but still this was my way of showing my care so I continued.

Every chaturti I went temple to get double benefit.. *Aarti ki aati attend karo aur thichi nazar se use dekho.*

After Aarti when the Prasad was distributed he made it a point to distribute it himself. He knew it with the same Prasad I would break my fast & if it's given with his hands then it's a cherry on the cake for me.

That night in between our chats when we were talking about breaking my fast with the Prasad he gave he complimented me "....its difficult to find such good girls these days"

..KIDS SHOW COMIN UP

Navratri was going on but I had no time to catch for dandiya. All day I used to spend time in practicing with kids & seniors for our performances. I often used to get so packed with work that I would forget Aarti timings but Vihaan, my Mr. rescuer always reminded me on time & I would make excuse and run down. His society was just a door away from my classes.

All nine days I would run down for Aarti & then he would make frowned faces if I got late or was messy.

My seniors expected too much from me. I was the only student who cleared all levels within 6 months & was appointed as a trainee & gave performances with the special batch.

They wanted me to be a part of belly dance as well hip hop for the show with handling my students' performances & our opening group dance.

It wasn't difficult for me to mange but then Vihaan didn't like when I did salsa or belly dance. He felt uncomfortable and that made me uncomfortable when I had to answer my senior's questions for not opting for belly dance. It wasn't like I didn't care about his likes or dislikes, in fact that was all that mattered to me but then professionalism was something that I had to respect.

Finally I came up with the only conclusion that I'm going follow my heart & do what Vihaan won't mind. His happiness was my happiness…
BLUSH!!!!!

Hip hop was lined up with other tasks but no belly dance. Perfect, I was all set to tackle the seniors.

With all things in place I met him in the eve & again special moments were on track.

Next day practices were on, belly dance was diverting my mind but then love was above all. I spoke to him on the way to home & He realized my restlessness so just came on the road opposite to my home in that freezing cold so that I could feel better.

Isn't this guy crazy??

... CHEAP PEOPLE TRY FLYING HIGH BUT FALL DOWN MORE PATHETICALLY.

While I was cross checking all my work before packing for the day Sanket sir approached me & started blabbering in front of all trainees' that I like him, keep starring at him & concentrate less on work etc etc.

Bloddy hell, who is he to judge me in this way. Whatsoever, he is my senior & isn't he here to have a professional relation with me & not this & who told him that I'm crazy about him & all. People like him have no other work than praising themselves when their good for nothing. Someone needs to tell him that I'm already committed to the best guy & we are going quiet strong but anyways for such men why should I open up my private matters. Let him fly high, soon he shall get what he deserves. I pity Rini & Meenal who have to work with him for maximum time & fall into his wicked traps.

..EMBARRASSING SECRETS OPEN UP

There were some folded secrets that I was yet to share with Vihaan, I couldn't back off from the thought of unfolding the fact of my life but then I didn't know how I should tell him everything.

That day was going to take our relation to a different level. I spoke to him about the bitter past when my uncle tried to clean his hands over me. With every tear I dropped & every word I uttered Vihaan held me more closer & more tight.

..COMPETITION DAY

With special batch I had participated in dance completion to be held in an engineering college. it was pouring out of season & mum didn't allow me to ride till the venue. Either I had to arrange passes on end moment for mum so she could accompany me or go with mit to the venue. The second option wasn't right choice as that wouldn't be accepted by Vihaan but then arranging passes was also impossible. Going alone by rick was the option instead of going with Mit but mum was not comfortable in sending me alone so I had to listen to her & go with Mit.

I informed Vihaan & he got upset just the way I expected but what was unexpected that he wanted to break up if I went with Mit. I wish I could stay back from the competition but then that wouldn't be fair to other participant s. I was often thrown into situation where my verdict never worked & then by abiding with other people's verdict I suffered all the unbearable pain.

That competition & that sleepless night fell like a thunderbolt over me as I was going to lose him again. I decided to quit dance once the kids' show was done. I had to give my dreams if I wanted Vihaan's love by my Side. Next morning I felt my last night decision was right & may be there is something better in store for me so I have fallen into this situation.

I called Vihaan n' number of times to talk & clear last evenings messes between us & push away heartbreaks. But he just avoided me & punished himself by staying in a lonely place where no one could find him crying. I also ate super spicy food to punish myself for hurting the one who loved me like mad. Filmy scenario was happening with the filmy girl, I was crying & the skies accompanied me, getting wet i started walking in the parking lane, alone, bare feet. I was just trying to figure out what I could so that he would talk to me. I was lost. I didn't feel the breeze too. It was like I was statue, who looks good but has no life. After getting wet for an hour or more coincidently I could see a ray of sunshine. And that was a positive sign for me. And there came a call from him, as the phone was buzzing I felt a bit better. I had to hear some taunts but then if he is talking I'm ready to hear anything.

Somehow I managed to convince him to meet me. My crossed fingers had worked again. We were together but the distance was like two strangers walking together. I had to take a step to get things to normal as I couldn't afford losing him so I just hugged without a second thought. We were with each other after a terrible fight and that was the indication of true love that fights negativity for the right thing to happen.

This was the closest moment when I felt him going away from me. God forbid, we would never walk on this path again.. Ever ever again.. Till the last breath I hope.

.. ONE MORE LIFE
ADDED TO OUR LOVE

We were back together after a nightmare so it was time to celebrate by spending some good moments but then my profession created gaps between us.

Next day when we met at *Cloud 9* after rescheduling other commitments to spend quality time there were some new hindrances coming up. There was a group of cheap guys so he took a U turn and we went for a short ride. When we came back I got a hug & before something else could happen we could see cop van so ride 2. Ride 3 & one of his friend saw us together & his bike zoomed to 80-100 speed and before that he told me to hug him tight as he was going speed up. Like this we had 4-5 rides to & fro from Cloud 9. While he was riding I just said sorry as I felt he was going to land up in trouble cause of me, there his nose turned red and he got angry but before he could say anything I just pushed a piece of dairy milk & that kept our him calm. ;P

Finally we grabbed a moment where we could sit peacefully and talk. That was the first time when I took a first step to kiss him & that too on the bike & I gulped the chocolate piece out of shyness instead of sharing with him.

..29 Nov

K ids show.. Time for every trainee prove their true abilities on stage, in front of overwhelming audience. I spent every moment of that day with care & collected as many memories as I could as this was the last day when I was with dance. After this it wouldn't have space in my life as Vihaan was going to take its place. Hectic day so didn't talk to him & he too didn't mind because he wanted me to make the best of these moments & before leaving get all the flying colors attached to my name.

I had dressed up like a kid with short skirt & hot top. Performances rocked my students performed up to the mark. I got the best compliments I could. Ma raised her head high with the proud feeling of having me as her daughter. At the end I walked on the stage as a trained model unlike others, this was the compliment given by the best kathak dancer I have seen.

It was time when my family was happy & he was about to see me in that outfit. He loved it. I entered his society premises with ma. As the chatting started, his friends also started commenting who had no clue about our relation.

"Trisha, you're looking hot & sexy"

"Thank you so much sweetheart. I thought you would get angry if you saw me in such an outfit"

"You just looking mind blowing; obviously I'm jealous as my friends also commented about you."

"What they said?"

"She is looking hot."

"Hahaha chill jaan & I'm sorry"

"It's ok, they are like that only & anyways you came here so that I could see you like this not for any other reason. But next time except me no one should see you like this."

"Possessive…."

"I have all rights to have that feeling"

"And I'm happy you have that feeling."

..CAN I GET A NAME TO THIS RELATION OFFICIALLY???

Out of nowhere problems cropped up at home. Mum is very angry as I'm paying off nothing to them after all possible talent in me. They want me to be on my own but I have not been able to do it after trying till the edge. When I couldn't speak up these issues with anyone else I thought of my diary, without any expectations or questions It always stood beSide me to grab in my pain, share my smiles. My mind is just speaking out one thing, my parents.. The named relation isn't working but the unnamed relation with Vihaan is going so strong. Why does this happen?

It's time when I want to get our relation official acceptance but this isn't that easy. Inter caste relation.. Different cultures & beliefs', will parents give agreement to it?

God this is the time when I feel like there isn't any point in surviving if I can't have my love beSides me forever. None of my dreams are showing up in reality. I want to give up & end all desires. No me=No desires

..BEFORE BIDDING GOOD BYE TO THE YEAR I SEND SOME PRAYERS WITH IT

A nother year came to an end but I wasn't as happy as I should have been. I'm more scared & worried. I hope when this New Year, a promise comes over that I will stay with Vihaan forever with our parents blessings. A promise of a life long relation with the guy who brought colors of love & happiness into my life.

He is the guy who makes me smile as I see him, has heard my shouts, wiped my tears, held my hand when I was lost, let me bump into his arms and made me feel secure, pampered like a mother, yelled like a father *(he & my dad's thoughts are synonymous).*

We two wanted to spend a life together holding hands to never leave again but then we had to think about our parents. A moment without each other sucks oxygen out of us & entire life without each other would shatter us to never get normal. He promised if our parents don't agree to our relation we would be friends, the best ones but is it that easy??

I can't hear him talking about some other girl then how can I see him spending a life with someone else.

Time had come when his parents were planning to get him engaged as his bro was also getting engaged. I knew this was about to happen but not so soon. We thought this would happen when we both would reach a stage where we could keep our point of view in front of our families.

I thought let's talk to our parents but then he didn't find this idea appropriate. I couldn't give up over this relation so easily, I trusted god always so left all over to him. Destiny would do the needful.

I'll put in my efforts wherever needed.

..THE LEAP MONTH

E xams are here... my boards were so not happening. Parents aren't as strict as him.

I need to plan about his birthday. I have picked all that I could. My parents didn't accept my salary so I had saved it & this was the best reason to utilize it. This is o not happening I have lost all my concentration, just can't study. finally somehow I clear my exams & there comes his birthday.

Me: hey dear where are you? Need to meet you up.

Why? Anything urgent?

Do I need a reason to meet you?

Actually I won't be able to make it up today. Li'l busy.

I'm sorry but I want to meet you in any case. Eve 6.30 I'll be waiting at Gera junction & I'm sure you won't disappoint me.

I'm not going come.

You'll be there I'm sure.

I was supposed to give him the t-shirt I got for him the day before his birthday so he could wear it the next day but it was difficult to convince him as he was quite smart in reading my mind so blackmailing was the best option for me.

Where are you?

I actually left as you were not on time.

Hahaha if you say so come back whereas the fact is you haven't come here.

Fine I'm coming.

I gave the t-shirt

it's not going fit me.

what are you serious?

Yuppzz. This isn't my size.

ok. Cool I can get a bigger size. I guess(still bitting my nails)

Relax aajayega, stretchable hai na.

Are you sure? Did you like it?

I hope. Ya baba its nice.

All set. I recorded happy birthday song for him in my voice & was just waiting for the clock to strike 12 & there goes the birthday greeting message with the pre-recorded song.

Thanks a lot dear. This is was the best wish I could ever come across.

Me: the best person has to receive the best,. isn't it?

I got up a li'l early compared to other days. With other surprises I had to make something cooked by my own self to make him feel more special so I started making gajar ka halwa. Mum dad were quite surprised when I started working on it, they wondered why I was doing this as it was very rare when I got up early & that too started cooking something I never tried my hand on before.

Let me tell you, when we eat gajar ka halwa we don't realize the effort & time & love spent over it by our beloved mothers, but when we actually make it we almost start sweating in the very beginning.

No doubt I went through the same but then I was smiling too cause then it was going land up in that someone's hand whom I loved the most & moreover this was the first time he was going taste something made by me.

Finally I was done with the cooking, winded all other work. By the time I was supposed to meet him I was almost dead tired.

Hey dear wassupp where are we meeting?

I doubt it's possible. It's moharam & our area is blocked.

It's ok. I'll come somehow. You just tell me where are we meeting?

Stay home.

Nope. I wana meet you. Upar se ma pa bhi pimpri jaa rahe hai.

Cool. I'll come home then. Best option.

Me: rubbish. I know you won't come.

I'll come pucca.

I'm leaving. Give me a call in next ten minutes & tell me where to meet.

ok madam.

He picked me from college but I still didn't have any clue where we were heading.

Where are we going? I asked

Carnival. He answered

Carnival? But then this isn't the way. We were suppose to go in the opposite direction isn't it?

Yeah madam your right but then do you mind spending more time with me, going for a long cut instead of shortcut way?

Nupzz. Not a problem at all. In fact I would love to.

That's better & anyways I don't have license for a gear bike. Remember? And after the German bakery blast incident the checking on those ways is more strict.

Chalo blast se muje kuch toh fayda hua. Blushhh

Fayda?

Yeahh… long ride plus remember we weren't talking when you were in Bombay & when the blast occurred you were the first one to text & get worried about me.

So Is that bad?

Areee aisa kab bola maine??? That was one more point when your concern was visible.. Acha listen…I'm sorry kyun re?

Actually with this cake I had ordered for a bouquet with 18 red roses but then that dumb fellow fell short of flowers ☹

You're dumb not that fellow. Bach gaya main.

Huh. What was that?

Dumbo where would I keep those roses?

That's bad, mere feelings ki kadar hi nahi hain.

Ha kya. You're spending time with me isn't that enough for you? Sheee mood spoil kar diya.

Oye don't say that. I didn't mean that.

Chillax just kidding. Kitna jaldi dar jaati hai.

Obviously.. tujhe manana is like walking over a hill top. Never easy.

So finally here we are.

Itna jaldi.?

Madam apki chattar –pattar me time ka pata kaha chalega?

Ha toh nahi karni chahiye kya.. chattar pattar..

Abi chal andar.

We walked in but then this time he just went ahead & I found it a li'l weird. What I mean is last when I came to carnival with him we walked in with holding hands & otherwise too we walk together but this time nothing of that sort happened. A deep breath & just walk in, he might be tired of riding.

So here comes the cake with HAPPY BIRTHDAY JAAN written on it. He cut the cake & mr smart had the entire piece where jaan was written. He didn't like celebrating birthdays but then I was just hoping now on he would like it. He told me that Manoj & Shilpa were also going to join us. I wanted to spend time with him but then it was good to hear that sooner or later I was meeting someone related to him. All four of us spent good time together. Manoj started talking about our future plans, how we would talk to our parents about it, some suggestions etc. That did piss him off but luckily Manoj didn't notice it. He switched the topic to his love story which was quite interesting. Everyone had the gajar ka halwa & liked it too. While we were leaving Shilpa questioned are you sure about this relation? Are you sure that he will talk to his parents about you? What if he doesn't take a step? I had nothing to answer her except that let him decide what needs to b done next, I'm sure he will take the right decision. The day wasn't great but it was one of those moments that we shall treasure.

..TOTALLY UNENEXPECTED DECISION.

As my exams were ending I could see him drifting away from me. I didn't know the reason behind it but then it was hurting. At first I thought may be its just my assumption but then when he didn't make any plans of meting up after my last exam I took my thoughts a little seriously. Evening we were just talking & indirectly I tried figuring out what's the matter but then we landed up fighting. I could hear murmur where one of his friend said why are you getting so hyper?

I had no clue what was he up to & then suddenly he said I want to break up with you?

It was like saying that all the time we have spent together was just a mere dream. I tried talking to him but then he just avoided. After disconnecting the call I just went back to all the times we had spent & I just recalled the way we entered carnival. For that second I felt since his birthday something was coking in his mind but just cause of his exams he stayed numb.

I felt helpless & out of frustration tried to cut my nerve but then it didnt work & I just got some scratches.

Few days later I spoke to Kanika & told her everything that happened & she got upset with my silly act.

Kanika: I know he means a lot to you but then what about your family? You think if he gets to know all this he will come back or be calm? Obviously not so just control your emotions. If it is meant to be then it will happen or else you need to let it go.

I knew I had taken a wrong step but then it was just an act out of absent mind.

In another fraction of seconds he Vihaan texted out of concern & I summed up everything & told him all that occurred. As expected he was very upset.

Vihaan: what are you trying to prove? I don't think you love me. Cause if something would have happened to you, your parents would have caught me & then we both know what would happen. And what would I answer my parents? Good I ended things but I swear your heights. Such immaturity is unexpected.

I was left speechless as I knew I was wrong but then the mistake was committed & nothing be changed.

We never spoke after that.

..GUJARAT HERE I COME

My vacations had started & I didn't want to stay in Pune as it was obvious for us to come across & I couldn't bare the distance between us. So I spoke to ma and left for Gujarat asap. the day before I was leaving I didn't have a control over myself, tears trickled down continuously. Mom figured out something was wrong with me & kept questioning but my voice was choked. I spoke to my bestie jia & told her that before leaving I'm going tell mom about my relation with Vihaan. It's high time when I stop hiding things from her. As planned I told mom everything but unexpectedly she was calm & composed & it was difficult for me to digest that. The reason I gave her for our break up was a silly fight over ego.

She just said two things to me, I'm your mother & I know what goes on with you & what all you do so never think you can hide anything from me. I noticed the blush on your face when you saw3 him I can still see the love in your eyes & I'm very sure you will never forget him.

I was stunned when she mentioned.. *You will never forget him'*

With a heavy heart I was going away from home but I was happy mom knew everything. Before leaving I left a voice message for him "no matter if we have changed our ways but then at any moment if you want to talk to me I'll be there. And I promise I'll never disturb you."

For the next 5 days I kept staring at my phone for his message or call but didn't make any efforts from my Side to call or message.

Sixth day I got a call from him. And it was obvious I was extremely happy. For a change there was a smile on my face. We spoke for hours like nothing had happened. Since then we got into contact again.

..VILLAGE ROOF TOP

I was back to Pune.& we met up in village. At first instance he sat opposite to me but later switched to the chair next to me. Poor waiter wasted 10 minutes over our argument when I chose salty lime juice & he ordered a sweet lime juice for me. The waiter didn't know whom to listen to, the guy next to me or me. With no option left he had to listen to him. He showed me images of his new house, while laughing over my recent pictures.

Vihaan: I wish I would have been there when you clicking this pic.

Me: why?

Vihaan: it looks like your just about to kiss someone.

I too muttered.. i wish I could kiss you now.

After spending quality time together when we stepped down, we just kissed and it was like,

The best kisses..
They are the ones you don't know are
happening..
The ones where you say goodbye..
Start to walk away.. And he grabs
your wrist, Pulls you back
He leans in and kisses you..
Those are best and the sweetest ones..
That actually make your heart race.

We patched up again.

..DAD'S ACCIDENT

When happiness knocks your door, it doesn't come alone. It brings in sorrows too. my relation was walking on untrodden roads when dad's accident happened. My entire family was relying on me as i was the elder daughter and dad conSidered me as his son & the one on whom i could rely on was not available but then i still had to be strong enough.

Massi & jiju had come down to see dad so it became difficult for me to handle as me & Massi never agreed together on an issue. But then main concern was peace at home and dad's health. With passing Time I adjusted to the prevailing situations. Meanwhile I missed out on Vihaan & it had a negative impact on our relation. This was the first time when I was not able to give him time & he was upset it. At one point he felt I'm not interested in him anymore whereas that was not the reason. After giving him continuous assurance with passing days, finally I got an ultimatum from him when he said I give you three days, mend things between us or else we'll part ways. The pressure started piling up. I blamed him for not understanding me but then he wasn't wrong, our relation needed attention. I tried my best to give him time but then it wasn't like before as family issues were priority. Giving me some concession Vihaan added two more days to get things on track but nothing worked on my part. I could see strings between us losing its grip & I was helpless, I couldn't differentiate between him & family. We didn't end up but a jerk came up. I was given time to handle family & rethink over the relation. With baby steps we were moving ahead.

..ANOTHER BREAK UP ON ITS WAY

As I was just trying to settle things I planned for a movie so we could spend time together but didn't know it would turn into a mess. Usually he was fine with anytime I opted for, but this time it wasn't that. He was more concerned about the college hours & restrictions so I had to reschedule the movie hour. I was happy cause it was the time I would see him after a long time but then on the other hand it wasn't the same. We were watching the movie but as strangers sitting together. After the movie I got to know mom had restricted him from talking to me. *How many times I would have to go through this?*

Once more it was time to follow parents so I was left alone standing there as I saw him go away from me. After that we just had a small chat on my birthday, that's it.

..SAD NEW YEAR

As I was back to phase one, it was difficult for me to do anything without him beSides me. So just to pull out my frustration I started dancing again that I stopped because he didn't like it. I took classes for kids & diverted my mind. I started talking to Danish (distant cousin) whom Vihaan personally didn't like & always felt he would approach me some day forgetting our actual relation, but I never felt so cause Danish was much obsessed with his career & involved with his friends where I didn't fit. He was just a good friend for me with I could share stuff related to me & Vihaan. On an unusual occasion Danish asked me out to attend a party with his friends. I assumed it was something related to his course but then I didn't know that it was specially arranged for me to get some time to hold on to him & get over Vihaan. I was shocked when I got to know this. After that I felt uncomfortable but couldn't find a way back home. I thought of calling up Vihaan but it was almost 12 am & then I thought Vihaan wouldn't feel good if I was seen with Danish. So with that uneasiness I passed some time & I was home.

A day before I Vihaan's birthday I saw him, just to act I'm doing well without him I overtook him & next day didn't wish him to make him realize my importance in his life.

..March

Vihaan just hopped back in my life from nowhere. I was surprised to see his number flash on my phone. He needed some notes & knew I would have them. Without thinking about all the sour memories I rushed to give him that. After a long time we met but it didn't take us long to talk our hearts out. I told him about Danish & the party; instantly he responded I would I come if u needed me. *blush*

His exams were approaching and I said I'll be there if you need help as I got an off from exams cause I wasn't allowed to sit for long as I met with an accident & spinal injury had occurred.

Meanwhile Nani got paralysis attack, mum dad had to rush leaving me alone to handle bro's exams & spent a colorless Holi.

Vihaan had exams but we stayed up late till dawn and chatted for hours & spoke about all mischievous things a girl & guy could. Missing out sleep was worth it.

Mum dropped out of house again during summer vacations to see Nani. Vihaan went off to Goa with friends but then the distance didn't come in. he spent more time talking to me instead of getting lost boozing or loitering on beaches.

For the time I saw him feeling enthusiastic about getting something for me on his way back to Pune.

Vihaan: You like to wear Payal or Anklets?

Me: Both.

Vihaan: Okkkk

Me: Hold on why all of a sudden you're asking this?

Vihaan: Just thought to get you one.

blush

When he came back he came empty handed. Apologizing I couldn't understand which one you would like so didn't get. But no problem we'll go out some day then you can pick what you like.

That's ok. The thought was more important.

(brain talks: I would have liked anything you would have got. When we were dating this never happened toh ab kya hoga.)

..FALTU

JUST FOR YOU, cause just thinking of you only brings a BIG BLUSH on my face...

Vihaan said our friendship will be just hi bye kind of but I wanted our previous friendship.. The one we had before our relation started but he said it's not possible but later he did that ... the old lovely friendship was back... I was happy and he too... we went for Faltu.. That movie was just an excuse to spend time together.. when we exchanged a glance in the parking and the first word that came to his mind was SEXY... it was just amazing.........his compliments still did made a difference to me..i promised him nothing will happen between us but while we left he got closer..i didn't even realize when he hugged me...then the rest.. I didn't wanted to move away but a promise is a promise.... but at certain level we just followed our feelings not practicality. Then the fun we had in the parking was just great.. Sometimes hanging between two relations is good that's what I felt that time... I was between 2bf's.. boyfriend and best friend......as a best friend I could tell him everything and as a boyfriend I could do a li'l mischief with him.. Hold his hands.. Feel his touch.. etc etc...that was really memorable.... after that I had plans to go out for a ride with him.. I knew he wouldn't have said no.. but Jia madam called and all went hay way, but still it was a good evening.

..DAY OUT WITH STUDENTS.

After a tiring picnic I was just relaxing when I had a fight with dad over a silly issue which later turned out to be a big one that left mom & me to leave the house & go to my grandparents place. I thought, quietly I would move away from Pune to Gujarat...but didn't have the strength to do so.. Wanted to hide the situation that happened at home so I avoided Vihaan & Jia all day but finally I had to behave as all is normal and talk otherwise his extra smart would smell something fishy & understand everything even when I stay quiet..I met him.. Thinking that I'll feel better if I talk to him and for a while hi sahi I'll be able to come out of the last night trauma but he read my eyes hidden behind the specs. I told him everything as I never conSidered him as an outSider. I knew there isn't any solution he could provide but still it was a relief speaking up.

..BEAUTIFUL MOMENTS

There were some hours left for me to depart with mom to my grandma's place but before that saying a last good bye to Vihaan was a necessity. Since he knew the entire story he stayed in constant touch & didn't give me a moment where I could fall weak. All of a sudden he planned for a movie to spend last moments together as I wasn't sure when I would come back to Pune or will I come back to Pune?

This gesture meant a lot for me so I made an excuse at home saying I'm going out for lunch with friends.

Today when I recall that day it's much like confusion. I was sad as I was going away from him but then I was happy because the moments we spent were never like before nor have happened till date. That day all I could feel is, *tere hone se main hu, main hi main hu, tu hi main hu....* W e didn'tsee the movie as we were completely lost in each other. While leaving instead of having tears I had a cheek to cheek smile thinking about the moments we spent in those 3 hours.

..EMOTIONS TAKE OVER

S eeing your parents depart is like a nightmare but I could experience it. Trust me it's the worst experience. I wanted to run back to Pune & make things better for my family.

Somehow after staying there for 2 weeks I paved my way back home. I convinced my cousin to get me back and luckily he agreed. I was staying at my aunt's place & my entire luggage was my grandma's place and without bothering about that I came back with the 2 outfits I had carried to my aunts place. This showed how desperate I was to come home. I hadn't informed Vihaan about it, so I had a chance of giving him a surprise. But bad luck he saw me before I could do anything & the worst part was he wasn't all that happy to see me back. In fact he thought going Gujarat, no chance of coming back etc was a drama. I was totally shocked seeing such a reaction. He didn't believe how difficult things were for me since I was going up to the real escape. Clearing things for him was turning burdensome.

..CRY OVER SPILT MILK

When things started falling in place something had to fall apart. With timeless attempts we were holding on to each other when my distant aunt told me that Vihaan's mum blamed me cause of his cigarette & loitering in his old society. She felt I was the one who made him do all that. She was unaware of the fact we were no more going around & I was the one who tried my best to keep him away from it. This wasn't the first time when I was being misunderstood but then this time it had cut down my patience & decided to talk about it with Vihaan.

The discussion turned into an argument as I couldn't control my tone & he couldn't bare this. I felt sick for always being at the gun point. This time I walked of leaving behind a sorry note. The fight piled up after I said you're good for nothing, you don't have the guts to talk to your own mom. When you can't face her then how dare you try to teach me something & eventually he decided to return all the gifts & end everything.

.. A LETTER

I had seen him in a friends party. Vihaan felt jealous when I danced with him so he smoked more than he could. When I was home all I could do is write this & mail him but then I just wrote it down…

HI DEVDAS,

What are you up to yaar, I know you love pool but not at the cost of losses, having drinks but not at the cost of such drunker look, your personality every person appreciates but take some time off & look at the mirror ….that's why this is the latest name I have given you "DEVDAS".

Jo mujhe dukhi atma bolta tha aaj use kya hua hai. Kyu wo aise ban gaya. Sabse door kyu ja raha hai. Har baat par shak kyu??? I mean why????

Fine accepted we are no more friends but in past we were close friends and we did share a close relation too, then why today you get so frustrated with my name that you argue with your friends. Have I hurted you or said something that wasn't right. I guess no, then why you hate me so much. Don't talk to me but at least don't hate me.

And stop blaming the common friends we share, they are not the one to give me updates about you… c' mon its logic and sixth sense… For 3 years I have been with you… I know you that well that I know what you do, when you do etc…

And don't act as if you don't remember my number also… one message and you reply W HOSE THIS…I mean don't reply that's better rather than hurting like this. Don't try to act in front of me. How could you tell Karim to date me????? Best friend ki aur X - GIRL FRIEND ki koi value nahi hai... as I got to know this I wasn't shocked cause you have done this before too in Angels n Demons 'you did show me some guys... but I felt bad for such trust of yours on me and Karim. BTW your after lines melted me... as usual still your care was reflected when you said take care of her, be with her till she's fine when you knew that with all this mess and confusion in my life I would be stagnant but you should remember that it was just you with whom I feel complete, with whom I can share every bit of my life and no one else. Mom gave you swear not to talk to me and you did it... good you followed her words but why didn't you do the same when she said about your smoking. That time you broke her swear and still you do smoke...

Doesn't that matter???

Last time at Adlabs nothing was intentional, I was hurt to know that still mom doesn't trust me... I mean I always tried my best to keep you away from things like excess pool, regular hookah, cigarette that are not good for you. Even mom wouldn't like to see you with all these things.

But then she took me wrong. It's ok if she judges me in a wrong way, it isn't her fault cause she doesn't know me but you did, right? I always conSidered her important, treated her as my 2nd mom and she will stay the same, always. I didn't stop talking to Rupal cause of you. It was just that with right time I got to see her real face. So better don't blame yourself.

Exams here, study well single backlog means a year down. Don't waste time.

It's high time you grow up.

..NO CONTACT

I made an attempt in December to get back but failed.

Since the last bickering we never spoke till his birthday. I was attending a friends' marriage in Bombay so told Karim to take the cake delivery & celebrate Vihaan's birthday on my behalf. Vihaan knew the idea behind the scenario was mine & denied to accept the cake at first instance & acted angry but inside he felt good. As a routine I gave him a call & wished him sharp at 12 by reciting happy birthday for him.

I was contented that we were still connected inside even when we didn't see each other.

I had heard of love and its magical stories and often dreamt of having one.

Then you bounced in my life with a key to my heart to give me a whole new refreshing set of happiness and made me feel how perfect it felt to be loved.

LOVE CAN NEVER HAPPEN TWICE

L ife had been changing a lot those days. Ankur was getting on my nerves. I got all what I expected from a guy, but 1 thing lacked on my part. I could never feel for him the way I felt for Vihaan.

He liked me genuinely but I was creating distance between us. I had just messaged him, wishing his mum as It was her birthday.

But then he came up & started chatting. He was quite disturbed with life & things that were told to him about me.

I appreciated he was still concerned about me & my life.

We started talking & sorting matters. He was still not opening completely. But I didn't mind as I directly couldn't pull him out of his comfort zone.

As I still believed in climbing the stair case step by step rather than jumping and falling into a cliff.

His presence in my life mattered more than the relation we were sharing.

He directly never told me about his feelings but I always caught the hints I got.

As I liked to spend time with him, talk to him for hours, chat without bothering about time, *ek jhalak ke liye taras jana.* He too liked the same.

Slowly his actions were doing what he was avoiding. i wanted him to meet me on my birthday as that was the best ever gift I could get. His time mattered for me. He avoided a lot but still he came & met me. We spent 2 hrs together.

That day everything was completely new & for first time.

Earlier we never had a walk for miles together or shared my fav chaat (panipuri). But that day we did it all.

There were some people who still couldn't see us together so they did try creating differences between us, but trust is something that didn't fade between us. We still knew each other & other people's comments didn't bother us.

He said I don't want the world to know about our friendship, but then he sent me a friend request on face book.

I couldn't understand why he stepped into the shoes that didn't fit him. He simply replied, "I know I'm not doing anything wrong then why should I worry & jo hoga dekha jayega."

..SAME CLASS

As new term starts I started hunting for taxation class. As said earlier when we were a couple we made a pact that henceforth we would join same coaching class & college to get a chance to spend maximum time together. But that never happened as our new term started on sour note. After waiting for years that time came, he wanted me to join taxation classes with him. Undoubtedly I said yes at the first instance. Since then spending time after class eating each other's brain was the only task we had. People around were shocked to see us together like this & commented that we are back as a couple but we gave up on bothering about them long back as we were happy in our own world.

But then as his home was just walking distance we realized it wasn't safe for us to wait there so we shifted to a park nearby where we wouldn't be spotted by commentators' or parents.

Since my birthday things had changed drastically, he had started taking initiatives to meet up, talk, spend time together.

For a change I saw him speaking up & loved to hear him without disturbing. Usually a girl's voice mesmerizes the guy but here the scene was different. More or less I had exchanged roles with him in this love story ;p

Other than pulling each other's leg, fighting over petty issues we had serious talks too. At one instance when I questioned why all of a sudden he peeped back in my life, the answer was one of the least expected. It went on as '*when we parted ways there was a time when I felt lonely. I had people around but I never could speak up to them. At times I sobbed too. But now it feels great to have you beSides me. I can share things with you.'*

Going for dinner was another turn we came up to. Let me admit I messed up our first dinner date. Out of conscious mind I ordered spicy food which he had it with a nice big smile but later puked out as spice was not a part of him. I really felt sorry that day.

Every time the blush on my face explained my friends my happiness & they often exclaimed. You both are two fools, madly in love with each other but just deny the fact and call yourselves just friends. By the way you should be knowing what just friends mean, right? You have read that novel too. Apart from all this 14 Feb has gone, why you didn't go for dinner that day, why after that?

When friends tease you, when your
face is flushed with color of love, even
the sunny day seems bright & coldest
weather turns warm.

..A NIGHT WE SHALL NEVER FORGET

My picnic was scheduled on his birthday & I was super irritated. I didn't want to miss out so I waved off the idea to go. Seeing this he lied to me that he also won't be in town as he was going Gurgaon was his snooker tournament. I wasn't convinced as this day was coming after a long time.

As fate always walked with me my picnic was rescheduled to a day after his birthday. His gifts were in place, he was informed I left for the picnic. I wished him at 12 with a pre-recorded poem written by me & said sorry for not making his birthday special to make him stay away from assuming what's coming next.

Evening I just called him by saying I'm back so let's meet up, lucky me I wasn't bombarded with questions like – how come you're in Pune? You were supposed to be in Konkan. etc

I kept him perplexed and confused between the time we spent going for rides & dinner. That was the first time I saw him like that. We shared coffee at the same old CCD to recall old memories.

Candle light dinner was set. He got his gifts one by one after a break of ten minutes each and every time the waiter came with something his eyebrows rose in suspicion. The best gift was the keychain he got. He said once, it looks like it's you're birthday & not mine cause you're so much more excited than me. And I felt you're not less than a part of me. I'm here because of you. I got the best return gift, a snap clicked with two of us after 5 years of knowing each other.

..SILLY ASSUMPTIONS

I was back in Pune. My friend had made an excuse saying she can't drop me home so he came to pick me up. She assumed we would roam around as I had no deadline that night but plans shattered as he thought his parents were already home. But getting his glance after coming from a short trip was just perfect.

Since that day he stopped meeting up as he thought I would get drawn to him again or let me correct it by saying I was infectious for him as he knew if he stuck around me, then it would be difficult for him to go elsewhere.

Silly guy didn't know that I had crossed all limits & nothing was left. He was all I wanted, whether he was around or not.

..ICICI TRAINING

E xams were about to start, so I dumped myself into hectic schedule with books & ICICI training sessions. Exchanging looks in class was all that happened between us. I couldn't see him drifting but it was his call & I couldn't help it. But during exams when I lost calm I saw him right beSide me, not concerned about what anyone else felt instead just concerned about my comfort..

..MOVE ON

" Trisha, have lost your senses again. When Vihaan left a year ago you somehow managed to be stable, you became firm about everything, and you stopped hurting yourself with expectations. But now look at you; you're again falling into the same mess. Don't. Please stop it. He doesn't care about you. He talks to you only when he wants to, otherwise you're just an option. Stop wasting your time on him. I know you can never forget him nor you will but at least you can try. You have to do this or I'll call up Vihaan & tell him he is good for nothing & is just using you. Think about your family, career not him." Jia gave me this never ending lecture. On the other hand some random guy told Pari that Vihaan was just doing time pass with me & he was getting along with someone else. I knew both my friends wouldn't lie but then my never ending trust on him didn't fall weak.

..PATIENCE TESTED AT PEAK

Trisha is still waiting for Vihaan's head to turn. She got her call letter from ICICI. She is about to move out of the town for it. Obvious, she doesn't want to go but doesn't have a choice. She can't stay without her family, friends, most importantly Vihaan. She aspires to be with him & stay with him forever but Vihaan is yet to realize what she feels about him or maybe he fails to understand his emotions for her. She stops sharing her feelings with him as she doesn't want any sympathy, but the moment he calls her fake she blurts it out. She tells him that she did all that so he doesn't has to stay numb when she says I love you & wants to be with him forever at his will but even then Vihaan doesn't respond to it. Instead he tells her to move on by dedicating *'bhula dena muje, hai alvida tuje.. tuje jeena hai, mere bina'* from Aashiqui 2 & she reverts by dedicating him *'tu muje chod jaye ye nahi ho sakta..'* same movie.

It's difficult for her to forget him & get a new life. But her friends are looking forward to it, so that she finds a person who deserves all her care, love etc. They will miss her but don't mind a little distance for her better future. Some of her friends wish that Vihaan should hold on to her before he loses her in the crowd.

..ICICI

Finally with a heavy heart Trisha pushed off Vihaan and started concentrating on her upcoming job in ICICI.

Obvious, her friends supported her totally but none noticed the depth her heart sank up to when she spoke carelessly about Vihaan with all sourness to make all believe she was absolutely cool without him. She didn't pay any attention to him till he made an attempt to talk to her & when she interacted with him all that reflected was I care a damn about you attitude. With this behavior too, Vihaan knew she was just acting whereas he still mattered to her.

But till she didn't show he never asked. Luckily Trisha got settled in Pune itself with her job after waiting for 2 months of velapanti with Samir and Shashank.

They both irritated her, made fun of her, made her laugh and dance. Instead of Vihaan they both sticked to her mind. This all happened with the grace of Pari. She brought them in her life so Vihaan's thoughts could be flushed off but then as clock striked Pari and Trisha realized Shashank and Vihaan were similar in many aspects and at equal in intervals she missed Vihaan badly when Shashank stayed in front of her. Four of them knew this and Shashank felt sorry for the same but was helpless. With them she felt pampered a lot so she warned them not to do so as this could turn her nasty but they ignored.

For Samir after Pari Trisha was important. His official duty was to make her smile.

HER BDAY..

O ctober was here.. Trisha was turning 21... She loved the feeling of growing lil older.. lil more mature. She was hoping for some surprises. Loose talks with Vihaan made her expectations pile when he just muttered that he will meet her at 12. She gifted her ownself a smart one piece saying let me do some exceptional out of the box stuff.

The d day was there. Calls texts had begun. Mum, choti nani, Pari, mit had filled her room with gifts already before 12 so she started unwrapping them

Samir kept her hooked on call so he could grab the chance to wish her first and he did get it.

Vihaan arrived... she wanted to go down and meet but he acted strict and didn't let her get down. A heart to heart talk shared while she kept demanding a scheduled long meeting and smart clean shave... She loved her teddy like that.

Her phone beeped.. *Happie birthday beta god bless u..... may all ur wishes may come true..... except 1* - Samir turned up home with Pari next morning with cake and trophy that they won recently. He knew Trisha would go crazy seeing her dream trophy in her hand. All day was great with family and friends. She missed Jia but wanted Her to walk up to her. Vihaan wasn't well so she turned restless. Her day was incomplete without him so she insisted on seeing him. Once again she rode and he sat behind her.. In shivering cold she felt cozy. As per her demand he went against his will and let her try beer. Usually she scolded Vihaan for boozing but that moment she wanted to be a freak

Her day was perfect

After that date she started being more demanding. On the contrary Vihaan liked it. Office work was getting messy. Sudrela Sashwat and I started interacting and akdu Amey and I fought like dog and cat. I started hating him and he got jealous cause I jelled with Shashwat. Stupid mentality was expected from staff.. They thought I'm playing double game with Rishi sir and Sashwat and all this happened because I smiled at the one who smiled at me and gave frown looks to those who were irrational and judged me otherwise.

One occasion I and Vihaan landed up at a pool parlour. He promised, he would do all that I demanded this was scene 2 after beer pact.

He tried teaching me to play pool but that wasn't my cup of tea. I just enjoyed getting his attention. He played with someone else & won too so I named him champ thereon Long drive and panipuri were next on the list and he bowled them.

..STRESSED.

O ffice was part two stress of her life. She gave her best but was left behind the rest.

No one believed her capability and she too was losing her confidence. Amey was turning the devil in her life. She hated him just as much she loved Vihaan. She was getting closer to Vihaan again and Shashank Samir were pushed to one side.

Obvious Samir was upset and equally worried as he didn't wanted her to keep hopes with Vihaan but fact was she did.

SHOCK OF HER LIFE.

Pari and Vihaan became friends and started interacting more than expected and as Pari cared a lot for Trisha so it was obvious something was bound to happen that she cracked something to get her smile long lasting.

The day came when Vihaan picked Trisha's novel and thought of reading it and realized that Trisha was losing herself in his love. Sanket his best friend too read it and made Trisha feel obliged for her art.

Pari had already read the book and was driven by its craziness.

Vihaan wouldn't have even thought of this, but Pari made him to do it.

She punched him with such heavy questions that he opened up in way that made shocked her.

She had to face Trisha and tell her to stop her be positive attitude and she did it.

"Vihaan never loved you. It's his care that he stuck around you these 5 years. He read your novel and the impact has been so powerful that he has decided to move out of your life so that you deserve right things in life.

He is guilty as he isn't able to give you what you expect. He cares for you like no guy can but can't give you the love you want.

Trisha was dead. Her love was stabbed. She felt rejected, guilty, lost, undeserving. Three nights her tears were her life but she smiled for Vihaan, Pari and her family.

No one could notice her pain. She acted but Pari and Vihaan knew what was happening but then wanted her to accept things as soon as possible.

It didn't take time to things go wrong when Trisha moved away from Vihaan and Pari both, as she felt it was good to stay alone rather than be with people who can't see you sad.

Thereafter, for silly reasons she fought with Pari not knowing why. Suddenly she asked Vihaan to be with her on 8 Dec, their 5th anniversary of their so called relation to end things on sweet note. They spent good time together as she wanted.

He took her to cloud 9 as she loved that place and the memories they spent there.

.. TWIST

S he is prepared for her cousin's marriage and the proposals that her parents have told her about. She is firm that she has to keep up to her parent's expectations and will say yes if the guy matches up to her expectations (super tough as she is bound to compare everything with Vihaan) but she is trying. Meanwhile Amey and their relation have turned pinch better. They have started knowing each other and started understanding each other. While she is out of town he is more interactive than she could have been with Vihaan. Both have been avoiding each other for betterment of each other.

She rejected 2 proposals as they were not what she wanted.

Unexpectedly she came close to Rahul's family and they loved her and then Rahul, loved her too. She thought of it but then gave up with the thought as settling in Ahmedabad was not for her and Rahul was not that bold guy who could handle her.

POST MARRIAGE.

A mey and Trisha got really close. Entire office noticed it. Vihaan Pari hated it but never uttered a word. Samir poked her directly.

Pari's closeness with Vihaan started bothering her as whenever three of them met she felt not needed.

She couldn't see anyone closer to Vihaan no doubt she trusted them. She took this threat and tried walking little more away from Vihaan.

CLARIFICATIONS....

Trisha was running away from Vihaan & Pari so they could share their pains and feel good and she could move on but then both couldn't see that.

They kept her shuffled. Nor they let her be rude, selfish, and mean nor did they let her be sweet, demanding, and loveable. She was sick of dual life. Bluttered out in anger that turned everything sour.

AGAIN FEB WAS IN A MESS....

Vihaan added her to reject list. She skipped his bday surprise. Shashank's family accepted Pari as their daughter in law and she was busy dealing with future planning.

Vihaan ringed up Trisha and scolded her for skipping his birthday and showering ego. They made each other realize that they can't bare ego clashes. Vihaan accepted that he was possessive about her and didn't like if she shared things with someone else that's' why he blocked her. He missed her on his birthday.

..Trisha Vihaan ki adhuri kahani.

After not seeing Trisha for a month he calls her up, she fights back as this time she wants to remove all her anger no matter how he feels. All that matters is having transparency. He accepts all mistakes committed. Promises to speak all he has in his heart. She meets him after ignoring 5 back to back calls. He accepts that he loves her, likes her but has big dreams of being self dependent, owning a big house where they stay together. A range rover to drop her to her parent's home and hi-buza to take her on dates.

And can't make her wait till he achieves all of them as he can't be selfish.

She is flattered again. She is listening all that she wanted to. Moreover she can see him being self dependent.

ROYENGI YE AANKHE,
MUSKURANE KE BAAD,
AAYEGI RAAT DIN DHAL NE KE
BAAD!!
RUTHNA NA HUMSE,
SHAYAD ZINDAGI NA RAHE
TERE JAANE KE BAAD!!

WHEN WE REALIZE THAT OUR RELATION IS GOING TO END WITH SOMEONE WITH WHOM WE WANTED TO STAY TOGETHER ALL OUR LIFE THEN WE TRY EVERYTHING TO STOP THAT FROM HAPPENING AND WHEN EVERYTHING FAILS WE REQUEST TO MEET AT LEAST ONCE... ONE LAST TIME... WHEN WE MEET WE ASK TO KISS ONE LAST TIME.. A FINAL KISS.. HAVE YOU EVER TRIED TO FIGURE OUT THAT WHAT MAKES US ASK FOR THIS ONE LAST KISS ? IT'S A BELIEVE THAT THIS FINAL KISS WILL MAKE YOUR LOVE RECALL ALL THE TIME YOU BOTH SPENT TOGETHER, THIS ONE LAST KISS WILL CHANGE YOUR LOVE'S DECISION TO GO AWAY... AND THIS ONE LAST KISS WILL BE ENOUGH TO KEEP YOU BOTH TOGETHER AGAIN !!

I CAN STILL REMEMBER YESTERDAY, WE WERE SO INVOLVE IN A SPECIAL WAY. AND KNOWING THAT YOUR LOVE MADE ME FEEL SO RIGHT. BUT NOW I FEEL LOST, DON'T KNOW WHAT TO DO. EACH & EVERYDAY I THINK OF YOU, I MISS YOUR SMILE. I MISS YOUR KISS. EACH & EVERYDAY I REMINISCE. CAUSE LETTING YOU GO IS NEVER EASY, BUT I LOVE YOU SO THAT WHY I HAVE SET YOU FREE. I KNOW SOMEHOW SOMEDAY I WILL FIND A WAY TO LEAVE IT ALL BEHIND WHEN I SHALL TAKE MY LAST BREATH. GUESS THIS WAS MEANT TO BE. BUT BEFORE I LEAVE I WANT TO SAY I LOVE YOU, I HOPE YOU ARE LISTENING COZ ITS TRUE.

IF I LOVE YOU MORE THAN
ANYTHING ON THIS EARTH
THEN DON'T BE SURPRISED.
THIS IS THE LEAST YOU
SHOULD GET FROM ME.

IF I VALUE YOU MORE THAN
MY LIFE THEN DON'T WONDER,
THIS IS THE TINIEST FORM

OF YOUR WORTH.

IF I GIVE YOU ALL MY
HAPPINESS & WISH TO TAKE
ALL YOUR SADNESS, DON'T
APPRECIATE..THIS IS WHAT
YOUR EXISTENCE DEMANDS.

IF I COULD, I WOULD HAVE LOVED
YOU EVEN AFTER I HAVE DIED
BUT I KNOW IT ISN'T POSSIBLE,

BUT UNTIL I'M ALIVE, UNTIL I
BREATH UNTIL MY SOUL IS IN
MY BODY, I WILL LOVE YOU

I GUESS ITS DESTINY...

EVERY TIME YOU LOOK MY WAY,
MY HEART SKIPS A BEAT.
IT FEELS LIKE LOVE TO ME.
TOO BAD THIS FEELING IS JUST
A SECRET.
YOU DON'T FEEL THE SAME, IF
YOU DID, THE WORLD WOULD
BE PERFECT AND EVERYTHING
WOULD CHANGE.